The Carpet Boy's Gift

Pegi Deitz Shea   Illustrated by   Leane Morin

"I appeal to you that you stop people from using children as bonded laborers because the children need to use a pen rather than the instruments of child labor."

–Iqbal Masih, 12 years old, from his Reebok Youth in Action Award Acceptance Speech, Dec. 7, 1994

TILBURY HOUSE, PUBLISHERS GARDINER, MAINE

Master says I have only two more months until my peshgi is paid back. With that thought, Nadeem quickened his knotting of the scarlet weft threads on the loom and then beat them tightly into place with his panja. I'm sure Master means it this time, Nadeem hoped. He must mean it.

Nadeem pictured himself free, playing soccer with his little brother Hakim. In the daylight! Since his parents had to sell him three years ago for a loan of 1,000 rupees, Nadeem had worked in the carpet factory from dawn to sundown, seven days a week.

"Nadeem!" Master commanded. "Time to load the rug."

Wheezing, Nadeem hopped between the other carpet children who worked in the small dim factory.

"Lucky," muttered Amina, the tallest girl.

Nadeem grinned proudly and squeezed his cousin's shoulder. This was the third straight month that Master had chosen him to load the truck.

Nadeem stepped out into the blinding sunshine. "Ahhh," he said, filling his
lungs with fresh air free of woolen dust. As he helped Master load the rolled carpet
onto the truck, Nadeem stole glances at the colorful chaos of the marketplace—
bundles of sugar cane stalks, herds of jostling goats, huddles of jabbering traders.

At the end of the road a beautiful red and gold flag rippled above a building. What flag was that? Nadeem could not help his curiosity. Maybe he'd walk by there before he headed home.

Master's voice pierced the din. "That's it, Nadeem. Back inside."

It took a while to readjust to the gloom and dust of the factory. Nadeem stepped around the other children, hunched over like barley sacks on the charpoy platform. Reaching his own loom, he squatted, picked up the knife he used to cut the rug's threads. A violent cough escaped and made the dangling yarns sway.

Nadeem put his fist to his lips to muffle the sound. He remembered what had happened to the girl next to him. When she had started coughing blood weeks ago, Master sold her to another factory far away from her family. Nadeem couldn't bear living without his father, mother, and Hakim.

That night Nadeem and Amina took a different route home, past the building with the red flag. Nadeem ran his tired fingers along the raised letters on the sign on the wall, wishing he could read the words.

"My father said it's a school," Amina said.

Hearing the children's laughter and seeing the bright electric lights inside, Nadeem said, "School sounds fun. Do you ever wish you could go, Amina?"

"Sometimes," Amina said, "But it is impossible for us, so I try not to think about it."

Nadeem gave her a hopeful smile. "Maybe when we have paid off our peshgi."

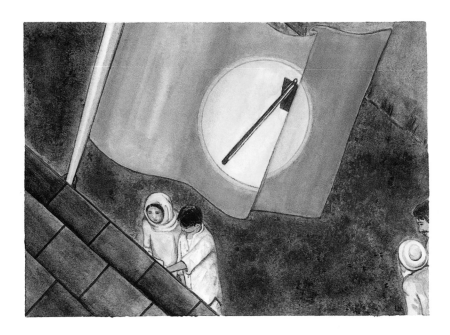

The next day as the children gathered to eat their midday meal Nadeem heard loud chanting outside. Master was in the back room, so Nadeem quickly peeked out the doorway. Softly, he called to Amina and the other children to come see.

"Amina, look—the same red flags," Nadeem pointed out as the children and adults paraded up the street.

"We are—?" called a boy leading the parade.

"Free!" answered the children behind him.

"We are—?" called the boy marching closer.

"Free!"

"That's Iqbal Masih," Amina whispered. "He used to make carpets, too."

"What does he do now?" Nadeem asked.

"I don't know, but I heard he flies all over the world in airplanes!"

Now Iqbal had reached them. "Come out!" he said, his voice high, yet ringing clear as a goat bell. "You don't have to work. You are free!"

Frowning, Nadeem took a step forward to meet Iqbal. "What do you mean 'free'? Master bought us for a fair price. When we earn back our debt, then we are free."

"No, you don't understand," Iqbal said, pulling out some certificates. "These are Freedom Letters. There is a law here now against child slavery—the law is called the Bonded Labor Abolition Act."

Nadeem fingered the papers and looked cautiously over his shoulder. "Master says we work for our country, for our families."

"Your master lies! He ignores our laws!" Iqbal replied quickly.

How could this be? Nadeem argued with himself. Master has been good to me—just this morning he let me load the truck. Isn't he honest? And who is this Iqbal? How does he know so much? Staring into Iqbal's eyes, Nadeem raised his voice. "How do I know you are not a liar?"

Iqbal carefully took Nadeem's hand and moved his fingers across the scars on his own hands. Both boys could feel each other's scars from their work at the looms, cuts healed over with boiling oil. Then Iqbal said, "My family needed money, so they sold me when I was about four. I escaped for good from the carpet factory work when I was ten."

"Hey, what's going on?" They heard Master yell from the back room. "Get to work!"

"Wait!" Iqbal said, and he pulled out a yellow pen from his pocket. "Here is a gift for you. A pen, not a knife, should be your tool. You can go to this school down the street and learn to read and to write."

Nadeem's mind tumbled. "I don't know."

"You can do it!" Iqbal said and handed Nadeem the yellow pen and some of the certificates. "Give these Freedom Letters to the other children. Present them all at once to your master. And talk to your parents. It will help if they come with you."

That night Nadeem showed his parents the yellow pen and told them about the new law and the school.

"But the master says we still owe him money. He might hurt us and take Hakim too," his father said. "It's very risky."

"Could we move to a different town, where Master couldn't find us?"
Nadeem asked. His father bowed his head and shook it while his mother held
Nadeem and his brother close.

Later, huddled with Hakim in bed, Nadeem couldn't rest his aching bones or stop his racing thoughts. How can I face Master? Shouldn't I wait just two more months until I've earned my freedom and I have paid off the peshgi? But I wish I never had to touch a panja again or tie another knot. I want to go to school and use the pen that Iqbal gave me today.

Then Nadeem remembered what had happened the first time he'd nearly

paid back his peshgi. Master had fined him 50 rupees more for falling asleep.
That took six months to work off. And the last time, Master fined him 100 rupees
for using the wrong color for only half a row. What would Master do this time to
make him work longer?

Feeling the breath of his four-year-old brother on his face, Nadeem sighed.
If I don't do something now, Hakim, you'll be knotting the threads beside me.

In the morning, Nadeem awoke in darkness as usual. His mother boiled millet for him and wrapped up some bread for him to eat later in the day. "Here's a bite for Amina, too," she said cupping his chin and adding, "Be careful, my son."

Nadeem hid his pen in his pants seam and hurried to the factory to get there early, before Master's clock said five o'clock. As the other carpet children arrived, he gave each one a Freedom Letter and explained what they would do. Amina's eyes glistened with excitement. Nadeem pressed his finger to her lips.

Soon, Master stepped out of his office to shout the instructions for the rug pattern. Nadeem had to clench his fists to calm his shivers. Then he stood and motioned the children to hold out their letters.

"Master," Nadeem said. "The law says we are free. You can't keep us here against our wishes."

Master's eyebrows pressed down as he walked toward Nadeem and snatched his letter. "Hmmmm," he said, reading.

"So it does say that. Did a boy named Iqbal give this to you?"

Nadeem bit his lips to keep from answering.

"We know all about Iqbal Masih. These Freedom Letters are worthless. And so are Iqbal and his friends." The Master ripped the paper in his hands into shreds.

As Nadeem watched the bits of the Freedom Letters fall like ashes to the floor, his heart beat wildly. He threw himself to the floor to gather the pieces. Master yanked him up. "Now you'll get a taste of what Iqbal should get himself."

"No!" cried Amina, covering her face with her hands. Master grabbed Nadeem's panja and dragged him into the back room.

Weeks later, shackled to his loom day and night, Nadeem knotted away
mindlessly. Master had fined him 500 rupees. It would take years to work it off,
and maybe years before he saw his family again. He didn't even look through
the door anymore when Amina helped load the truck. The light stung his eyes.
The fresh air prickled his throat.

One morning, Amina crept over, choking on her words.

"Nadeem, I just heard Master laughing on the phone because Iqbal went
back to his home town and he was shot dead. Iqbal's dead! Nadeem, do you hear
what I'm saying?"

Nadeem groaned. His hand touched the seam in his pants where he kept the

precious pen that was Iqbal's gift to him. Now was the time to help all the other children. That was what Iqbal had wanted to do. Nadeem pulled the pen from its hiding place and clutched it.

Nodding and shaking, Amina continued to cry quietly. "Master said, 'That's what Iqbal gets for freeing carpet children. See what his worldwide fame gets him!'"

"Shhh, Amina," said Nadeem in a calm voice. "I am making a plan."

Amina watched as Nadeem slid his yellow pen between the thick rope shackle and his ankle and gripped his curved knife.

Nadeem sawed back and forth against the rope, back and forth until the knife sliced through the rope that had bound him. Only then did he explain everything to Amina. Amina turned to tell the other children. She moved among the looms whispering, and then gathered the children near the door.

"It's time for us all to go," said Nadeem, standing.

"But I am afraid to go," a small child spoke up.

Amina took her hand and said, "Do you really want to stay here with Master?" The child shook her head.

"Iqbal was right," said Nadeem. "We don't have to do this work anymore. If we go together, the school will protect us. Look, its gates are open!"

Taking a deep breath, Nadeem stepped into the sunlight, in the steps of Iqbal, and all the children followed.

Because readers of *The Carpet Boy's Gift* often wonder what they can do about child labor, we have included some extra resources on these pages to help you understand more about this complicated problem. We encourage you to share these resources with your parents or teachers so that everyone gets to brainstorm ways to protect children's rights. The wonderful news is that any kid can help be part of the solution to make the world a better place for all children and families! Teachers will find further resources at www.tilburyhouse.com.

THE TRUE LIFE OF IQBAL MASIH

Iqbal Masih, the real hero who appears in these pages, was a boy from Pakistan. When Iqbal was about four years old, his family bonded him for a peshgi of about $12.00 to a rug maker near Lahore, Pakistan. Iqbal wove carpets twelve hours a day for six years years, working in bad conditions and suffering greatly from hunger and injuries, along with other children in the carpet factory.

One day Iqbal escaped and attended a rally held by the Bonded Labour Liberation Front (BLLF), an organization that was working to help children like him. He learned that a law against child slavery had been passed in Pakistan in 1992, but most factory owners didn't obey the law and the police didn't enforce it. With help from the BLLF, Iqbal began to sneak into hundreds of rug factories so he could educate other child laborers about

their rights. Many of the children Iqbal spoke with took their own steps toward freedom so that they could to go to school, get medical attention, and be protected by the BLLF. Iqbal himself was able to realize his dream of getting an education. He was a good student!

In late 1994 Iqbal was honored at an international labor conference in Stockholm, Sweden. Later that year he traveled to the USA, where he met school children and received the Reebok Youth in Action Award. Iqbal wanted to grow up and become a lawyer. He had the promise of a scholarship at an American college. But when Iqbal returned to Pakistan, people made threats against his life. On Easter Day, April 16, 1995, at age twelve, Iqbal was shot to death while riding his bike in his hometown, Muritke. Although Iqbal Masih was a Christian, his Arabic name means "Destiny Messiah."

Learn more about Iqbal Masih and other child advocates:

• Kids' Campaign to Build a School for Iqbal: http://mirrorimage.com/iqbal/

Read interviews with some middle school children who met Iqbal at Broad Meadows School in Quincy, Massachusetts. Learn how he inspired them to act on behalf of others.

• World's Children's Prize for the Rights of the Child: www.childrensworld.org

There are courageous kids everywhere who have made a difference working for the rights of children. This website has many profiles of kids like Iqbal who make a big difference working for children's rights. The prize is given in Sweden and some adults call it the Nobel Prize for Children. Offically it is called World's Children's Prize for the Rights of the Child.

• *Iqbal Masih and the Crusaders Against Child Slavery* by Susan Kulkin (Henry Holt, 1998).

This book describes the life of Iqbal, his activism against child labor, and how other people have continued Iqbal's work. Ages 11-14

Learn about the United Nations and "The Rights of the Child":

Imagine you had the responsibility of creating a list of children's rights for children everywhere! What do you think are the most important rights every child should have? What would you include? Brainstorm your own list of "Rights of the Child" with friends and classmates. Then, compare the ideas you think are important with the UN's official Rights of the Child, listed below.

This is the draft of the first set of rights for children all over the world. It was written in 1959. What do you think of these ideas?

1. All children have the right to what follows, no matter what their race, color, sex, language, religion, political, or other opinion, or where they were born or whom they were born to.
2. You have the right to grow up in a healthy, normal way, free and with dignity.
3. You have a right to a name and to be a member of a country.
4. You have the right to good food, housing, and medical care.
5. You have the right to special care if handicapped in any way.
6. You have the right to love and understanding, preferably from parents, but from the government when you have no parent.
7. You have the right to go to school for free, to play, and to have an equal chance to be what you are, and to learn to be responsible and useful.
8. You have the right to be among the first to get help.
9. You have the right not to be harmed and not to be hired for work until you are old enough.

Learn more about the United Nations (UN), its history, and the work it does for the rights of all children:
• United Nations Children's Fund (UNICEF): www.unicef.org

This is the homepage for UNICEF. This organization's first mission was to bring emergency aid to hungry children in Europe after World War II. Today UNICEF provides aid to children all over the globe. Their programs range from raising funds for Trick or Treat for UNICEF to work on clearing landmines in countries such as Afghanistan and Vietnam.
• United Nations Children's Cyber Schoolbus: www.un.org/cyberschoolbus

This is a UN website where kids can learn about global issues and social responsibility.
• The 1989 UN Convention on the Rights of the Child: www. childrensworld.org/wcpswe/childrensrights/engindex.asp

Visit this site to learn more about diplomacy. See what still needs to be done to get all member nations to agree to support and implement the Rights of the Child.
• *For Every Child* by Caroline Castle (UNICEF/Penguin Putnam, 2001).

This book identifies the most pertinent rights of children and it is written in language anyone can understand. Beautifully illustrated by fourteen children's artists. Ages 5-12

Learn more about the work the United Nations does on the issue of child labor:
• United Nations Children's Fund (UNICEF): www.unicef.org/aclabor

Take an interactive quiz at this UNICEF site so you can see how much you know about child labor around the world.

EXPLORING THE ISSUE OF CHILD LABOR

Child labor is not limited to Pakistan. In Ecuador, it's estimated that 69,000 kids pick bananas, while in the U.S. the estimates are that as many as 800,000 children may work illegally at farming and related industries. Child labor occurs in many parts of the world. The United Nations estimates that 250 million kids between the ages of 5-14 work. In many cases, the wages children earn help feed their families. But some countries have no laws to protect children from working long hours in bad conditions. A big question is what types of jobs are acceptable or unacceptable for children.

Understanding child labor:
• International Labor Organization (UN affiliated IPEC):

www.ilo.org/public/english/standards/ipec

This kid-friendly site will help you learn how much child laborers earn, what kind of work they do, and how much time they spend at their jobs. There are also links to many other useful sites on child labor and some ideas for action you can take to make a difference.

• Time Magazine: www.timeforkids.com

See what other children's news organizations write about the problems of child labor today.

• Scholastic News Zone: www.scholastic.com

This news site has lots of information, including a map of children in the labor force, country close-ups, voices from the field, and ways to help.

• *Lost Futures: The Problem of Child Labor:* www.aft.org

This 16-minute video from the American Federation of Teachers is updated every year and comes with a guide. $15 from AFT at 202-585-4361. YA

• *Listen to Us: The World's Working Children* by Jane Springer (Groundwood Books 1998).

This balanced photo essay looks at the hazardous work children do in developing and industrialized countries. Ages 9-12

• *Stolen Dreams: Portraits of Working Children* by David L. Parker (Lerner Publications, 1997).

Learn about young rug weavers, prostitutes, and migrant workers in Bangladesh, Thailand, Pakistan, the U.S. YA

• *Free the Children: A Young Man's Personal Crusade Against Child Labor* by Craig Kielburger and Kevin Major (Harper Collins, 1999).

This book is a call to those who want to end abusive child labor and poverty. The author founded Free the Children, a powerful organization in support of kids' rights. YA

• *The Kids' Guide to Social Action: How to Solve the Social Problems You Choose and Turn Creative Thinking Into Positive Action* by Barbara Lewis, Pamela Espeland, and Caryn Pernu (Free Spirit Publishing, 1998). YA

Learn about the history of child labor:

Throughout time children have worked in many occupations in all countries. In addition to reading about child labor, you can see photographs or videos in some museums and galleries. Check to see what's available locally.

• *Kids At Work: Lewis Hine and The Crusade Against Child Labor* by Russell Freedman (Clarion Books, 1994). Nonfiction

A wonderful photo essay that chronicles the state of child labor in the U.S. in the early 20th century. Ages 9-12

• *Working Cotton* by Sherley Anne Williams (Harcourt Brace, 1992). Fiction

A child's view of the long day working in the fields picking cotton in the American South. An introduction to migrant work. Ages 4-8

• *The Bobbin Girl* by Emily Arnold McCully (Dial Press, 1996). Fiction

Rebecca, a 10-year-old bobbin girl in a mill in Lowell, Massachusetts, in the 1930s, leads her co-workers out on a strike. Ages 4-8

• *The Gate in the Wall* by Ellen Howard (Atheneum, 1999). Fiction

An orphan escapes work in a silk factory in Victorian England and begins to work on the barges. Ages 11-14

• *The Adventures of Oliver Twist* by Charles Dickens (Oxford University Press, 1987). Fiction

The famous story of the poor orphan who lives on the streets of Victorian London. Ages 10-14

• Tsongas Industrial History Center, Lowell, Massachusetts: www.uml.edu/Tsongas/

The center has a hands-on exhibit where you can see how "mill girls" lived. The web site has activity suggestions and teaching resources.

WHAT'S THE BIG DEAL ABOUT EDUCATION? ARE ALL SCHOOLS ALIKE?

Why did Iqbal and the other children in *The Carpet Boy's Gift* want to go to school so badly? Why do you think school is important?

Do you think all schools are the same? You can discover the ways that schools are alike and different from country to country and continent to continent by finding penpals or using the Internet. A big question is: are all "educations" equal? What do you think makes a person have a good education? It's interesting to learn about the different lunches that kids eat and the books and lessons teachers assign. Do all kids get "recess"?

Explore life in different schools around the world:

• Epals: www.epals.com

If you have a question, this is the place to get an answer! 4.5 million students and teachers in 191 countries access this site to exchange information and ideas about their perspectives on issues large and small.

• Keypals Club International: www.worldkids.net/clubs/kci/

Find a penpal and share news and ideas!

Learn about schools and organizations that help former child laborers get an education:

• Free the Children: www.freethechildren.org

Learn about the Kids Can Free the Children School Building Campaign (KCFTC). 300 schools in poor areas of the developing world have been supported by this effort. It's very interesting to compare the pictures of some of the schools that have been built, with the pictures of schools that have made contributions to help.

• Rugmark International: www.rugmark.org

Rugmark supports schools for former child workers and works to have better standards for the working conditions in carpet factories in Pakistan, Nepal, and India. If your family buys a rug with a Rugmark label, then you know you are supporting efforts to help workers.

• Kids Campaign to Build a School for Iqbal: http://mirrorimage.com/iqbal/index.html

Learn about middle school children in Quincy, Massachusetts, who fundraised to build a school in Iqbal's memory in Pakistan.

• *We Need To Go To School: Voices of the Rugmark Children* by Tanya Roberts-Davis (Groundwood Books, 2001).

This moving book has interviews with former carpet children from Nepal. Each page reveals their stories as they reflect on the changes in their lives once they are able to go to school and leave their harsh lives behind. Interviews, poetry, and photographs give a powerful voice to the drama of these children's lives. Ages 9-12

Discover more kid-to-kid projects that help others:

• Global Art: A Sense of Caring: www.iearn.org/projects/senseofcaring.html

Put your feelings of concern to good use! Sign up to share your artwork and writing with other schools around the world. Uses both web and snail mail resources.

• Free the Children: www.freethechildren.org

In addition to the school-to-school projects, Free the Children provides children and their communities with medical relief. More details about the work this group does are listed in the section above.

WHERE DOES YOUR STUFF COME FROM?

All companies are not the same. Some treat employees very well while others do not. You can support good companies and learn to be a responsible shopper with help from adults and these websites.

Good Goods? Map the sources of your clothes and toys:

• Check the labels on your clothes and toys to see where they are manufactured and locate them on a map.

Compare the pros and cons of buying clothes or toys made in places where the labor practices are questionable. Use the resources below to get information on companies, and try to support companies who treat their employees well and work to make the world a better place.

• Responsible Shopper: www.responsibleshopper.org

Enter the name of a company and learn about how it is rated by human rights organizations and consumer groups. Especially good for kids and grown-ups.

• The Clean Clothes Campaign: www.cleanclothes.org or www.pica.ws/cc

Check this database to learn more about the clothes that you wear. Learn about the efforts of this group to make life better for people who work in sweatshops. Good for kids and grown-ups.

• Zillions Online: www.zillions.org

This *Consumer Reports* site is for kids, and it lets you rate toys and rides, talk about popular fads, and gives you a chance to give your opinion.

TILBURY HOUSE, PUBLISHERS

2 Mechanic Street

Gardiner, ME 04345

800–582–1899 • www.tilburyhouse.com

First printing: October 2003 • 10 9 8 7 6 5 4 3 2

First paperback edition: May 2006 . 5 4 3 2 1

Dedication—

• This book is dedicated to the memory of Iqbal Masih and to the courage of children everywhere. PDS and LM

• For the children of my hometowns, Matawan, New Jersey, and Vernon-Rockville, Connecticut. PDS

• For my family with love and gratitude: my sisters, Diane and Debbie, my late parents, John and Nan, and always for Kate, Sam, and Meg. A special thank-you to Genny, my "illustration fairy godmother." LM

Library of Congress Cataloging-in-Publication

Shea, Pegi Deitz.

    The carpet boy's gift / Pegi Deitz Shea ; illustrations by Leane Morin.

        p. cm.

Summary: Yearning for freedom and schooling for himself and the other children who toil in a carpet factory in Pakistan to repay loans from the factory owner to their parents, Nadeem is inspired by a former carpet boy named Iqbal to lead the way.

    ISBN 0-88448-248-0 (Hardcover : alk paper)

    [1. Child labor--fiction. 2. Rug and carpet industry--Pakistan--Fiction. 3. Child abuse--Fiction. 4. Masih, Iqbal, 1982-1995--Fiction. 5. Pakistan--fiction.] I. Morin, Leane, ill. II. Title.

    PZ7.S53755 Car 2003

    [Fic]--dc21

                                         2003008001

Designed by Geraldine Millham, Westport, MA.

Editing and production by Jennifer Bunting, Audrey Maynard, and Barbara Diamond.

Color scans by Integrated Composition Systems, Spokane, WA.

Printing and binding by Sung In Printing, Inc., South Korea.